For Grown-ups

About Communication

Communication is the process of sending and receiving verbal and non-verbal messages. It involves understanding feelings and recognizing that everyone has the right to express feelings without infringing on the rights of others. Children increase their skills and confidence as communicators when they receive the support they need to talk about what is important to them.

Parents can support their children to develop communication skills:

Talk with them: Give lots of opportunity for children to participate in conversations.

Listen to them: Recognize that what children have to say is important.

Respect them: When you consider your children's feelings they learn that everyone's feelings are valued.

Set an example for them: Surround your children with positive communication where ideas and feelings are expressed openly.

Guide them: Recognize that words are powerful and use positive messages when responding to your children.

It's No Joke, My Telephone Broke

By Linda Sky Grossman

Illustrated by Petra Bockus

Second Story Press

Hey, Amon, stop and wait up for me,

Let's sit for a while under that tree.

I want to tell you what happened today,

Just wait 'til you hear what I have to say!

School is a great place for us to be,

There's more to learn than adding one and three.

After lunch we were making so much noise,

The teacher called out, "ATTENTION, girls and boys!"

"I know that our work is almost done,

So let's play a game and have some fun.

Sit in a circle, instead of in rows,

Girl, then boy, that's how it goes."

"Broken Telephone is what we'll play,

Each must listen to what the other will say.

Cup your hand to your neighbor's ear,

Whisper the sentence that you think you hear."

"Niron, why don't you go first."

(He was so excited he thought he'd burst!)

Niron thought for a minute before he spoke,

The next person laughed, it was quite a joke!

Around and around the sentence was passed,

Some were slow and some were fast.

Some of the kids weren't paying attention,

Charlene and David are the ones I would mention.

At last the game came to an end,

It stopped at Vesna, you know, my friend.

The teacher said, "OK, now let's hear

What you've been whispering from ear to ear."

Vesna held her head up high,

And looked the kids straight in the eye.

"Butter tarts slide into the sea,

Is the sentence that was passed to me!"

Well, you should have heard the great uproar,

Kids were rolling on the floor!

Niron clapped his hands with glee,

"I said, Butterflies always fly free!"

Vesna looked down at the floor,

Tears stung her eyes and made them sore.

Why were the kids laughing at her?

She told me later, the room was a blur.

She only said what she *thought* she heard,

Perhaps she listened to a different word.

Vesna thought that her heart would stop,

She felt like an empty, crushed can of pop!

The teacher said, "Now that will do.

Vesna, we are not laughing at you!

This is a game, and that is it!

Laughing at others, I will *not* permit.

Sometimes children *listen*, but do not *hear*,

Adults also behave like this, I fear.

If you have something you want to say,

Be sure to speak in a very clear way!"

"If someone won't pay attention to you,

Talk to another, until *they* do!

Your thoughts are just as important as mine.

Speak out, you'll see, things will work out fine!"

"And now, kids, let's get back to our game.

Congratulations to Vesna, whom I'll name

Because of her courage in speaking out loud,

She is one great girl, no wonder she's proud!"

See what I mean, Amon, school is fun.

There are lessons to be learned by everyone.

While playing a game, we discovered something new,

Now I'll speak up, it's the right thing to do!

Hey, Amon, I think we'd better go.

My Mom will worry, it's late you know.

I want to tell her about our game today,

Who knows, maybe I'll teach her to play!

For all the great kids learning to speak out and speak up!

For Beth and Jack Sky, my mother and father, who taught me that education, once achieved
and the magic of imagination are two commodities that may never be removed from one's possession.
L.S.G.

For my sister Megan, who is always there for me.
P.B.

NATIONAL LIBRARY OF CANADA CATALOGUING IN PUBLICATION DATA

Grossman, Linda Sky
It's no joke, my telephone broke

(I'm a great little kid series)
Published in conjunction with Toronto Child Abuse Centre.
ISBN 1-896764-51-7 (bound).—ISBN 1-896764-45-2 (pbk.)

I. Communication—Juvenile fiction. 2. Self-esteem—Juvenile fiction. I. Bockus, Petra
II. Toronto Child Abuse Centre. III. Title. IV. Series: Grossman, Linda Sky. I'm a great little kid series.

PS8563R65I88 2001   jC813'.6   C2001-902232-8
                    PZ7.G9084It 2001

Copyright © 2001 Toronto Child Abuse Centre
First published in the USA in 2002

Cover design: Stephanie Martin
Text design: Counterpunch/Peter Ross
Printed in Hong Kong, China

Toronto Child Abuse Centre gratefully acknowledges the support of the Ontario Trillium Foundation,
which provided funding for the I'm A Great Little Kid project. Further funding was generously provided
by TD Securities.

Second Story Press gratefully acknowledges the assistance of the Ontario Arts Council and the Canada Council
for the Arts for our publishing program. We acknowledge the financial support of the Government of Canada
through the Book Publishing Industry Development Program.

Published by
Second Story Press
720 Bathurst Street, Suite 301
Toronto, ON
M5S 2R4

www.secondstorypress.on.ca